The #1 Sports Writer for Kids

Touchdown for Tommy

Little, Brown and Company

Boston   New York   Toronto   London

Library of Congress Cataloging-in-Publication Data
Christopher, Matt.
  Touchdown for Tommy. / by Matt Christopher — [1st ed.] Boston, Little, Brown, [1959]
        p. cm.
Summary: A young boy worries about making the football team and convincing his foster parents to adopt him.

  ISBN 0-316-13699-9
            [1. Orphans — Fiction.   2. Football — Fiction]
  I. Title.
PZ7.C458 To 1985

[Fic]   59-7340
                        20 19 18 17

                            COM-MO

            Published simultaneously in Canada by
            Little, Brown & Company (Canada) Limited

            Printed in the United States of America

1

Tommy Fletcher zipped up his black-sleeved gray jacket. He tugged on his baseball hat and stepped out of the warm house. The late September wind was bending the tall oak tree in the backyard. The clothes on the line whipped like a string of white flags.

A slip of green paper on the short-cut grass caught Tommy's eye. A ten-dollar bill!

Tommy picked it up. The money must belong either to Betty or Mrs. Powell. The three of them had been hanging the clothes out on the line earlier.

The last time Tommy remembered having ten dollars was long ago. Back in January sometime, before the terrible accident. Back when his parents had still been alive, before their car hit that icy patch of road.

1

But he was in a foster home now. Since he didn't have any living relatives, he had been brought by the child welfare department to live with the Powells. The Powells were very nice, but they didn't give him money the way his parents used to.

Tommy thought for a while. He decided that the ten-dollar bill wouldn't be missed by anybody. If it had been missed, Betty or her mother would have come looking for it.

Tommy put the money into his pocket. He walked down the long cement pavement to the highway. The only nearby store was over by the school. On both sides of the highway were houses — old houses and new houses. They were painted white, blue, green, and other colors. They were pretty, much prettier than the house Tommy had lived in in the city.

He passed two of the houses. Soon he heard the excited voices of boys. He knew at once what the cries meant.

The kids were playing football!

He started to run. I hope David is there, he said to himself. David Warren was the only boy in the whole bunch that he liked.

He ran past the store. Maybe he'd spend the money when he came back. A cold soda would taste good after playing a game of touch football.

Then his heart sank. He had forgotten to tell Mrs. Powell where he was going!

But why do I always have to tell her? he asked himself. I never used to tell my mother.

Well, it was too late to turn back now. He would tell Mrs. Powell when he got home. She wouldn't mind that he had forgotten just this once.

He turned to the right at the intersection. Up the road a little way was Barton Central School. Just this side of it was the large athletic field. The high school team had their own field, and the kids under thirteen had theirs.

The football field for the younger boys was all laid out like the high school field except that it was smaller. Instead of being one hundred yards long, it was eighty yards long. The bleachers were only on one side.

Tommy stopped running when he reached the field. Neither of the two teams had more than five or six players each. Maybe he would be given a chance to play.

He spotted David immediately. David wore shoulder pads under his yellow jersey and a red-and-white helmet. He was playing quarterback. The ball was on the thirty-two-yard line, and David's team had possession.

David barked signals. "Ten! Fifteen! Twenty-one!"

The ball spiraled up from the center. David caught it, tucked it under his arm, and sped around the left end. He made a gain of five yards before he was tackled.

As he rose to his feet, he spied Tommy. A grin spread across his face.

"Hi, Tommy! You want to play?"

"Sure!"

"Come on our side! They have one more player than we do!"

Tommy took his hands out of his pockets and rubbed them together. "Can I play end?"

"Okay. Play left end."

David motioned his team into a huddle. "Think you can catch a pass?" he asked Tommy.

"I think so," said Tommy.

"Okay. We'll pull a surprise on 'em," David said.

4

"I'll throw Tommy a pass. The number is forty-two. Let's go!"

The team broke out of the huddle. The backfield and linemen moved into position. Tommy crouched at left end and looked directly into the eyes of the end playing opposite him.

"Twenty-two! Fourteen! Thirty-six! Forty-two!"

Tommy sped forward. He knocked his opponent down and raced down the field. He looked back and saw David throw the ball. The pigskin spiraled through the air, wobbling just a little.

Tommy reached out. The ball hit his fingers then bounced to the ground!

"Yes! Incomplete pass!" a player on the other team shouted.

Another player picked up the ball and returned it to the scrimmage line.

"I'm sorry, David," said Tommy. "I should've caught that."

David waved his hand. "Forget it, Tommy. That was a tough one to catch." When Tommy was closer, David said, "Mr. Powell may stop by later on, you know."

Tommy shrugged. "Oh, yeah?"

"Mr. Powell's our coach," David continued. "He sure knows his stuff. We play in the Midget League. Be nice if you could play."

Tommy stared. "Do you think he'd let me on the team?"

"Sure, he would," replied David. "Ask him."

"I will. Maybe, if I can play real good —" Tommy paused. All the boys looked at him. Most of them had unfriendly looks on their faces.

Tommy knew they didn't like him much. He had scrimmaged against them before. They had said he was a dirty player. He played too rough.

But that was the way he always played. He didn't know any other way.

David's team tried another pass. It was intercepted. The opponents gained eight yards on line plunges, then lost the ball on a fumble.

First down, ten to go. David tried a run through right tackle, but failed to gain.

Again the teams crouched ready at the line of scrimmage. David called signals.

"Six! Thirteen! Twenty-two!"

The ball shot up from the center. David caught it and dashed toward the right end. A tackle broke through the line, reaching for David. David twisted and kept running.

He swept around the right end, crossed the scrimmage line, and gained six yards before he was brought down.

"Third down and four to go," David said in the huddle. "Dick, you carry the ball this time. Swing behind me and run around the left end. Tommy, make sure you take out your man."

"Okay," said Tommy.

David called signals. The ball came from the center to David. He ran toward the right side of the line, then suddenly handed the ball to Dick Mizner. Dick tucked it under his arm and raced toward the left end.

Tommy blocked out his man. But a halfback broke through and tackled Dick for a one-yard loss.

"Last down," David said. "I'll punt."

The team lined up in punt formation. David stood far back as he called signals. Then the ball sailed into David's hands. He kicked. The pigskin wobbled through the air toward the out-of-bounds line. The whole team ran hard down the field in the direction of the ball.

A player on the other team caught the ball. He ran forward with it. Tommy rushed up like the wind beside him. The player tried to stiff-arm him, but Tommy ducked his head and rammed his shoulder into the boy's body. At the same time, he wrapped his arms around the boy's legs. The boy went down. He hit the grass hard. Tommy hung on like a snapping turtle and rolled over with the boy.

"Okay! Let him go!" a voice shouted. "You gonna hang on to him forever?"

Tommy lifted himself off the boy. He saw the ball roll a short distance away. A player picked it up and brought it to the spot where Tommy had made the tackle. The boy Tommy had tackled rose to his feet. He limped around a little, and David asked worriedly, "You hurt, Jim?"

"No. I'll be all right."

Jim walked around a little more, and the limp disappeared.

"Tommy, you play too dirty," Jerry Main said gruffly. "Listen, David, I'm not going to play if he plays."

"Neither am I," said Ted Norton. "You'd think he was playing with some pro team."

Tommy's chin dropped. He looked aside at David Warren, met David's eyes. Dirty? What was dirty about tackling a guy? You had to tackle him so that he went down, didn't you?

"Don't be so rough next time, Tommy," cautioned

David. "The minute a guy's down, he's tackled. Didn't you know that?"

"Sure, but —" Tommy didn't finish. He had always tackled that way before. Nobody had ever told him that was the wrong way. Maybe these guys just didn't know how to play real football.

A car drove up to the side of the road and stopped.

"There's Mr. Powell!" cried David. "Maybe he'll stay with us for a while."

Mr. Powell stepped out of the car and walked onto the field. His gray topcoat made him look huge.

"Hi, Mr. Powell!" the boys greeted him.

Mr. Powell's grin was broad and friendly. "Hi, boys. Brushing up on some new plays?"

"Well, not exactly," said David, smiling. "We're just playing pickup. When is our first real practice, Mr. Powell?"

Mr. Powell chuckled. "Getting anxious?"

"Yes!"

"Well, the league starts a week from Saturday. How about tomorrow after school? Four-thirty sharp."

"Okay!"

"I'll stay to watch you run through a few more plays," said Mr. Powell. "Then Tommy, I think you and I will have to leave."

Tommy shot him a look, then nodded.

The teams lined up on the thirty-five-yard line. The team opposing Tommy's had the ball. They made a two-yard gain, then tried a forward pass. The pass was completed. The receiver was tackled on the forty for a first down.

Tommy played hard. He pushed his man aside and plunged after the ballcarrier with his chin set square as a box and his eyes flashing. He wanted to show Mr. Powell how well he could run and how well he could tackle. If Mr. Powell had played football in high school or college, *he'd* know what a good tackle was.

But Tommy didn't have a chance to show Mr. Powell anything except how hard he shoved aside his man and how fast he could run. Mr. Powell said it was getting late and he and Tommy had better leave for home.

In the car, Tommy remembered the ten-dollar

bill. He felt in his pockets for it. A chill went through him. He couldn't find it!

Mr. Powell backed the car out of the school driveway and headed for home. "Have you lost something, Tommy?" he asked.

"No. Guess not," said Tommy. But his face got red. He hoped that Mr. Powell didn't see it.

"You're quite a runner," said Mr. Powell. He grinned at Tommy. "Like football?"

Tommy was worried about the ten dollars. But he forced a smile. "I sure do. We used to play a lot where I came from."

"Did you play in a league?"

"No. We just chose up teams and played, that's all."

"You didn't have a coach?"

"No. We didn't need any."

The thought of the lost money drifted farther and farther away from Tommy's mind. He became excited talking about football. He tried to remember all the things about football he could. He remembered the time he had tried to tackle a boy and ripped off the boy's sweater. He remembered another time when he had purposely tripped a quarterback and the quarterback fell and hurt his knee. Those were things he didn't want to tell Mr. Powell, though. All he could tell Mr. Powell about were the times when he had caught long passes and had made long runs. But then that made him sound as if he were bragging, and he didn't like to brag.

They drove into the Powells' driveway, and Tommy asked, "Did you play football with a team, Mr. Powell?"

A light sparkled in Mr. Powell's eyes. "Yes. I played in college, Tommy. I was a tackle."

"Boy! That must have been great!" Tommy sighed deeply. A warm glow went through him all of a sudden.

Mr. Powell drove the car up to the garage door and stopped. Tommy jumped out and opened the door, and Mr. Powell drove the car in.

Mr. Powell came out. He put his arm around Tommy's shoulders. They walked toward the house.

"You've been with us about five months, Tommy," said Mr. Powell quietly. "How do you like staying with us? Have we been treating you right?"

Tommy looked up at Mr. Powell's face. He hadn't expected any question like that. He thought right away of his mother and father. A lump the size of an apple rose in his throat.

"I like it here a lot, Mr. Powell," he said, and swallowed. "You, and Mrs. Powell, and Betty — you've treated me wonderful. Just wonderful."

3

After supper Mr. Powell relaxed in the living room with the evening paper. Tommy sat in the kitchen. He thought about the ten-dollar bill. He must have lost it while playing football.

Finally he put on his coat and hat and grabbed a flashlight. "I'll be back, Mr. Powell," he said. "I'm going outside for a while."

He walked all the way back to the field. He decided on the way that if he found the money, he wouldn't spend it. He would return it to Betty or Mrs. Powell. Maybe if he did that, they would like him better. They would let him stay at their house for always. But suppose one of the boys had found it?

Tommy walked over the places on the field where he had run during scrimmage. He searched the ground carefully. The grass was cut short, but

15

looking for the ten dollars was like looking for a needle in the haystack.

He went to the spot where he had tackled Jim Neeley. Shining the flashlight ahead of him, he walked back and forth between the thirty- and forty-yard lines, his eyes glued to the ground.

He saw something flutter and picked it up, but it was only a wad of chewing gum paper.

Tommy kept looking. Then all at once he saw another bit of paper. It was pressed into the earth, half covered by the short blades of grass. He poked it out with his finger. It was the ten-dollar bill!

He started out for home with the money in his hand. He kept his hand in his pocket all the way. He walked by the store. Two cars were parked in front of it.

For a split second, Tommy thought about going inside. Boy, you could buy a lot for ten dollars. He felt thirsty, too.

But he went past the store and headed for home.

Betty was in the driveway, shooting baskets into the hoop above the garage door. She had on a gray, hooded jacket. She stopped when she saw Tommy.

"Tommy, where have you been?" she asked.

"At the football field," Tommy said. "I lost some money there and went back to look for it."

Betty's eyes widened. "Money? Where did you get it, Tommy? Did my mother or father give it to you?"

Tommy's heart pounded. "I found it in the backyard," he said truthfully. He held it out to her. "Here."

Betty shook her head. "Why don't you keep it?"

" 'Cause," he said. "It's not mine."

She looked at him thoughtfully, then smiled. "Let's go inside," she said. "I guess this is something for Mom to decide."

"I hope she won't be mad," said Tommy.

"Not Mom!" answered Betty.

They went into the house. Tommy heard a pounding in the basement. Mr. Powell must be working on the fruit shelves again. They found Mrs. Powell in the kitchen, a pile of papers spread out before her.

"Mom, Tommy found this money in our backyard," she said. "Did you lose it?"

Mrs. Powell looked at the bill in Tommy's hand. "I don't know. Did you just find it, Tommy?"

"No." Tommy swallowed. "I found it after we'd been hanging out the clothes this afternoon. At — at first I wanted to spend it. My mom and dad always used to give me money to spend. But I went to the football field and played football. I lost the money. After supper I went back and found it. I — I changed my mind about spending it. I wanted to give it back to you."

There. See what they would do now. Maybe they would call up Mrs. Kilbourne at the Child Welfare Department in Lewiston and have him sent to another foster home.

Then he saw a smile come to Mrs. Powell's face.

"Let's not worry about whose money it is," she said. "I think it was very nice that Tommy brought it back. Tomorrow both of you can go to the ice cream store and have a sundae each. How does that sound?"

"That's just fine, Mom!" cried Betty.

A warmth came over Tommy. "It's fine with me, too, Mrs. Powell," he said.

But deep inside he felt funny. He should never have walked away with that money in the first place. What if he'd blown it with the Powells?

4

Saturday morning Mr. Powell entered his football team, the Pirates, in the Midget League. First, Tommy had to be given a physical examination by a doctor. He passed with flying colors. His name was put on the roster, too.

Just before lunch, Mr. Powell brought home Tommy's uniform. It included a red-and-white helmet, a yellow jersey, pants, and shoulder pads. Tommy touched them piece by piece with his fingers. Each touch was a thrill. Then he put on the uniform. It fit him perfectly.

"We'll drive to Lewiston this afternoon," Mr. Powell said, "and buy you a pair of cleats."

Tommy could hardly wait. This was the first time he had ever worn a football uniform. He would be playing just like the bigger boys. With cleats he could run faster. And with shoulder pads he could tackle harder because he couldn't get hurt.

Tommy was glad that Mr. Powell was coaching football. Tommy would show him that he could run, throw, catch, and tackle.

He might turn out to be the best player on the Pirates team. If he did, Mr. Powell would really like him. He might even talk to Mrs. Powell and Betty about him.

"Tommy's the best player on the Pirates team," Mr. Powell would tell them. "I don't want to send him away. I want him to stay with us."

And maybe Mrs. Powell and Betty would agree!

All the Powells drove to the mall in Lewiston that afternoon. Mrs. Powell and Betty went together to shop. Mr. Powell took Tommy with him. They stopped in a sporting goods store, and Mr. Powell bought Tommy a pair of cleats.

"Now you're all set," Mr. Powell said with a grin. "We'll break in those cleats and your uniform after we get home."

The Pirates assembled at the football field at three o'clock. About twenty-five boys were present.

They all wore uniforms. Four footballs were being kicked or passed among them.

In their yellow jerseys the boys looked like autumn leaves blown around by the wind.

Mr. Powell explained to Tommy that the Lewiston Youth Bureau furnished the uniforms to all the players on every team and that each team was sponsored by an organization.

"Who sponsors our team?" asked Tommy.

Mr. Powell, who was wearing a heavy sweatshirt, smiled. "Barton Merchants."

Another man suddenly arrived in a station wagon. He was tall, about Mr. Powell's age, and wore dark-rimmed glasses.

"Hi, Bill," said Mr. Powell. "Meet the young fella I was telling you about. Tommy Fletcher. Tommy, this is Bill Adams, our other coach."

Tommy and Bill Adams shook hands. "Glad to have you with us, Tommy."

Tommy stared. "We have *two* coaches?"

Mr. Powell nodded. "Oh, sure. Some teams have three or four. The more dads we can get, the merrier."

Tommy thought that they would start scrimmaging right away. But he was disappointed. Mr. Powell and Mr. Adams called the boys together and had them do some calisthenics first. This took about an hour. Then the boys rested for five minutes. Tommy was glad for the rest. All those exercises had made him pretty tired.

He never knew you had to work out like *this* to play football!

Both coaches then picked out eleven players each and worked with them separately.

Tommy was picked by Mr. Powell to play left end. David Warren was quarterback.

"Let's practice a couple of plays," said Mr. Powell. "First, number twenty. David gets the ball from the center, twists around, and hands the ball to Kenny, who's running down from the right end. Let's try it."

The players lined up. David called signals. The ball snapped from the center. David caught it, turned, and handed the ball to Kenny. Kenny swept around Tommy at the left end.

"Fine!" said Mr. Powell. "Now let's try some passes. David, heave one to Tommy."

The players lined up again. Tommy's heart kept

jumping as he leaned forward, his right knee bent, the fingers of his right hand pressed against the ground. This was what he had been waiting for — a chance to show Mr. Powell what he could do.

David barked signals. Suddenly shoulders met shoulders. Helmets thudded against helmets. Tommy pushed his man aside and took off down the field. He looked over his shoulder. He saw the pigskin come curving down toward him. He leaped, caught the ball, pulled it against his ribs, and hung on to it tightly.

"Nice throw, David!" yelled Mr. Powell. "Nice catch, Tommy! Okay, try a pass to the right end this time!"

Exercise. Exercise. Exercise. Practice. Practice. Practice. The same thing took place on Monday, Tuesday, and Thursday. Exercise and practice.

"This is the stuff that will make you strong and fast," said Mr. Powell.

5

The Pirates played the Cowboys the following Saturday morning. All the games in the Midget League were played Saturday mornings because the high school team played in the afternoons.

Tommy didn't start the game. But he wasn't worried. Mr. Powell had told him that every member of the team would get in sometime during every game. It was one of the league rules.

The Cowboys won the toss. They chose to receive. Fullback Fred Wilkins kicked off. The ball sailed end over end down the eighty-yard field. A Cowboys player caught the ball, fumbled it, then picked it up again and ran it back to their thirty-three.

They gained six yards on a pass, then two more on a run through tackle. That put them across the forty-yard stripe on the Pirates' thirty-nine-yard line. Third down and two yards to go.

Another pass. It was completed! The receiver raced to the Pirates' twenty-five-yard line before he was downed.

A whistle shrilled. There were substitutions on both sides. Still Tommy didn't go in. He stirred nervously on the bench. He was anxious to play.

First and ten for the Cowboys. The ball snapped from the center. A pass! Another completion! The fans rose to their feet in the stands and roared. The runner was racing down the field. He crossed the twenty . . . the fifteen . . . the ten . . . the five . . .

Touchdown!

Tommy groaned.

The Cowboys kicked the extra point. Score: Cowboys 7, Pirates 0.

A whistle blew. The first four minutes of the first quarter were over. There would be a two-minute rest period, then the second four minutes would be played.

"Okay, Tommy, go in at left end," said Mr. Powell. "Send Jack out."

The game started again. David heaved a long

pass to halfback Tim McCarthy. It was intercepted! The Cowboys' player ran hard with the ball down the field! He was coming toward Tommy!

A player blocked Tommy, but Tommy pushed him aside and went after the ballcarrier. Just watch this tackle, he thought. Just watch.

The player tried to dodge Tommy. Tommy lunged after him. He ducked his head and swung his arms around the runner. His weight threw the boy to the ground. Tommy hung on and squeezed the boy's body so that he couldn't get away.

A whistle shrilled loudly. Then a pair of hands circled Tommy's middle and yanked him roughly away from the boy.

Tommy looked up into a referee's angry face. "Hey! Cut that stuff out if you want to keep playing! He's down!"

Tommy stared. He rose to his feet. He saw the disgusted looks of the players of his own team. What's the matter? he thought. How am I supposed to tackle?

A substitute replaced Tommy. Coach Adams motioned Tommy to sit beside him.

"Just bring the man down, then let him go," said the coach. "Play clean, Tommy."

Tommy wet his lips with his tongue. "Yes, sir," he said.

The half ended with the game still in the Cowboys' favor. In the third quarter David raced around the right end for a thirty-two-yard run to score a touchdown. Fred converted by kicking to tie the score.

In the fourth the Cowboys intercepted one of quarterback Jerry Miller's passes and raced for a touchdown that won them the game.

The whole Pirates team was noisy with excitement in the locker room as the boys prepared to take their showers. Even Mr. Powell and Mr. Adams were smiling. Tommy couldn't understand it. You would think that the Pirates had won the game instead of the Cowboys. How could they feel good when they'd lost?

In the car on the way home, he asked Mr. Powell about it, and Mr. Powell explained. "You see, Tommy," he said, "we play the game for fun. We try to win, yes. Everybody does. But that's not the most important thing. The most important thing is participation. Everybody plays."

There was a car in the driveway when they reached home. Mr. Powell drove around it and parked in the garage.

He and Tommy walked into the house. A woman was in the living room, talking with Mrs. Powell. She was a tall, nice-looking woman with glasses.

"Hello, Tommy," she said, the moment Tommy walked in.

Tommy blinked. "Hello, Mrs. Kilbourne," he said. To himself he added, What are *you* doing here?

6

How are your airplane models?" Mrs. Kilbourne asked. "Finished them yet?"

Tommy nodded. "Yes. You want to see them?"

"I'd love to, Tommy."

He hurried to his room and returned with the two models he had assembled from kits Mr. Powell had bought him. One was a swept-wing U.S. Navy plane, the Chance-Vought F7U-3 Cutlass. The other was a Navy jet trainer, the Seastar. The names were printed on the mounts on which the planes were fastened. Mrs. Kilbourne took the planes and looked at them admiringly. "They're beautiful, Tommy! You certainly did a very nice job."

"You can see the pilots, too," Tommy pointed out.

"I know," said Mrs. Kilbourne. "They look very real."

Mrs. Kilbourne was from the Child Welfare Department of Lewiston. She not only liked airplanes; she liked sports, too. Ever since Tommy had met her, and talked with her about things he liked to do, he had liked her.

"Do you want to speak with Tommy especially, Mrs. Kilbourne?" asked Mr. Powell.

"Well, I came to see Tommy, of course," she said. "But I would very much like to talk to you folks."

Mr. Powell nodded slowly. "Okay." He turned to Betty. "Why don't you put on your coat and you and Tommy go out on the porch for a while?"

Tommy carried his model planes back to his room. Then he stepped out to the porch. Betty was already out there. They sat on the red metal chairs.

"What do you suppose Mrs. Kilbourne wants, Tommy?" Betty asked.

Tommy shrugged. "I don't know. Maybe she just wants to know how I'm behaving."

Betty looked curiously at Tommy. "What has that got to do with her?"

Tommy stared at a crack in the floor. "If I wasn't getting along here, she'd find another home for me, I guess."

"Even if Mom and Dad wanted you to stay?"

"No. I don't think so. Only if I wasn't behaving and they *didn't* want to keep me.

They sat for a while in silence. They could hear Mr. and Mrs. Powell and Mrs. Kilbourne talking inside, but the voices were just a hum behind the wall.

What were they saying? Tommy remembered the money he had found in the backyard and had almost spent. He remembered the rough way he had played football. There were so many things he hadn't done right. Wouldn't he ever learn?

He rose and stood by the rail. A truck roared by. It scared a flock of sparrows off the electric wires. Far in the distance the sky was turning a deep red and purple and orange. Soon the sun would set and night would come. Tommy would stay up a little while longer, then he would have to go to bed.

The door opened. Mrs. Kilbourne came out. She put out her hand to Tommy. Tommy took it.

"It's been nice to see you again, Tommy," she said. "I'm glad to hear that you're enjoying yourself with the Powells. Mr. Powell told me you're quite a football player, too. I'm glad to hear that. I must get along, now. Good-bye, and good luck, Tommy. Good-bye, Betty."

Tommy touched his dry lips with his tongue. "Good-bye, Mrs. Kilbourne," he said softly.

He went into the house. He heard the car drive away, and looked at Mr. and Mrs. Powell.

"Am I going to stay here?" he asked, a lump coming to his throat.

Mrs. Powell smiled. "Oh, yes. You'll be with us for a while yet. After all, you're supposed to be with us at least six months. That means you're sort of on trial here with us. You remember Mrs. Kilbourne told you about that when you first came to us?"

Tommy nodded. "How long have I been here, Mrs. Powell?"

"Five months," she said. "So you still have another month, Tommy. But don't worry. We had a boy once who stayed with us for two years. It's all up to you, Tommy."

7

Tommy and Betty walked to school Monday morning. Betty kept talking about her arithmetic. Tommy hardly heard. Another month, he thought. Another month and probably Mrs. Kilbourne will take me away.

It's all up to you, Tommy, Mrs. Powell had said. But I *am* trying my best, he thought. What else can I do?

He was quiet in school. Ms. Bleam asked him if anything was wrong. He said no, nothing was wrong.

"Let's take out our reader," Ms. Bleam said, "and turn to page twenty-six. Tommy, will you start reading, please?"

Tommy found the page. He started to read.

"Please stand, Tommy," said Ms. Bleam.

33

Tommy stood up. "'One day Joseph arose early in the — in the — '"

"'Morning,'" said Ms. Bleam.

"'— in the morning. He ate —' um—"

"'Breakfast,'" said Ms. Bleam.

"'— breakfast, and walked down the road. He found a goose . . .'" He kept reading, missing words now and then, words he had remembered even last week, but which he could not remember now .

"You must study more, Tommy," advised Ms. Bleam. "Did you get a good rest last night?"

"Yes," said Tommy. "Yes, I did."

After eating his lunch, Tommy went out to the field with the boys to play scrub football.

Jim Neeley looked at Tommy. His eyes darkened. "If you're going to play, I'm going back inside."

"So am I," said Tim McCarthy. "Who wants to get a leg broken by a guy who thinks he knows how to play football?"

Tommy stared. "I — I didn't break anybody's leg!"

"No! But you're trying hard to!"

"Oh, stop that," said David Warren. He stepped between Tommy and the two boys. "Tommy never tried to break anybody's leg. He's always played rough because that's the way they played where he came from. They never played by rules. Don't worry, he'll learn the right way with us. But he can't learn if you don't give him a chance. Come on, Tommy. Play on my side."

They played till the first bell rang. Then they went inside.

That afternoon, when they returned home from school, Betty and Tommy found Mrs. Powell very happy about something. She was humming a popular tune and skipping from stove to sink to table and back again like a happy bumblebee. Her eyes danced. A couple of times she winked at Tommy.

"Well, Mom," exclaimed Betty at last, "are you going to keep us in suspense forever?"

"What do you mean by that?" Mrs. Powell tried to hide her smile, but she couldn't.

"You know what I mean," said Betty. "You're hiding something from us."

Mrs. Powell laughed. "Okay. I'll tell you. But it's especially for Tommy."

Tommy's eyes widened. "For me?"

"Yes. Mr. Powell telephoned me this afternoon. He said that when he comes home tonight, he'll have a surprise for you. There! You see? I shouldn't have said anything, Betty. Now both of you will be more anxious than ever!"

Every few minutes, Tommy looked at the clock on the wall. Mr. Powell arrived home each night about six-thirty. Tonight, the minutes just dragged.

Finally the car drove into the garage. Mr. Powell was home! And then the door opened, and Mr. Powell came into the house.

Both Betty and Tommy looked at him, and he looked at them. But he had nothing with him. His hands were empty.

8

Tommy turned to Mrs. Powell. Her eyes met his. They had just a touch of a smile in them.

"Mom said you had a surprise for Tommy," said Betty softly.

Mr. Powell's brows arched. "She did? Well, now—"

Suddenly a soft whimper sounded just outside of the door. The room was silent for a long second. The sound came again.

Tommy rushed to the door and opened it. He caught his breath. Right on the top step was the cutest little black-and-white cocker spaniel he had ever seen!

"A puppy!" cried Tommy. "A little cocker spaniel puppy!"

The pup's large brown eyes rolled up sadly at

y. His long, curly-furred ears quivered.
...my picked the pup up in his arms and brought
him into the house.

Betty screamed with surprise. "Let me hold
him!" she cried, stretching out her arms. "Let me
hold him! Ple-e-ase!"

"Wait a minute," said Tommy. "I just got him."

The pup was soft and warm against him. He
licked Tommy's cheek. Tommy laughed. Boy! A
dog! He had never had a pet before. And this one
was his. His!

"Oh, please!" Betty pleaded again. "Let me hold
him! Or is it a 'her,' Daddy?"

"It's a 'he,'" said Mr. Powell, chuckling.

"Betty," said Mrs. Powell gently, "I'm surprised.
You always said that you didn't care for dogs. We
wanted to get you one a long time ago."

Betty blinked a few times and clasped her hands
together in front of her. "I guess I never knew they
were so cute," she said.

Tommy grinned. He held the puppy out to her.
"Here. Hold him," he said.

Betty took him and held him close. The pup
looked around with his big sad eyes and blinked.

Mr. Powell pulled thoughtfully on his ear. "I probably should have brought home two dogs," he said.

"No. One is enough," said Tommy, smiling. "This one could belong to both of us — Betty and me."

"That's right!" cried Betty. "We both can have him!"

Tommy smiled. "We can take turns feeding him."

"Sure we can," exclaimed Betty happily. "We'll have to buy him puppy food and make a bed for him to sleep on."

"You'll have to name him, too," said Mrs. Powell.

"That's right!" said Betty. "Let's call him — let's see — Wag!"

"How about letting Tommy suggest a name for him?" said Mr. Powell.

Tommy thought a while. He looked at the pup's stubby tail. It was wagging back and forth furiously. Tommy grinned. "I think Wag is perfect for him!" he said.

"Okay. We'll name him Wag," said Mr. Powell.

Wag wiggled his long ears and turned his sad-looking eyes on Tommy.

Tommy smiled and hugged him very hard.

9

Mr. Powell found a box in the basement. Mrs. Powell folded an old quilt, placed it inside the box, and put the box in a corner of the kitchen.

"During these fall and winter months we'll keep Wag inside," she said. You could tell by the warmth in her voice that she loved the little fellow, too.

The words echoed and re-echoed in Tommy's ears. These fall and winter months? What did she mean by that?

Was *he* going to stay with them? Maybe the Powells knew. Maybe Mrs. Kilbourne knew. But *he* didn't know.

If he could only make the Powells like him. Really like him, so they wouldn't want him to go away.

* * *

"Mom," Betty said after she came home from school that following Monday, "can I stop at Kathy's house tomorrow after school?"

"Did she ask you?" asked Mrs. Powell.

"Of course! She said that her mother said it was all right. She wants me to stay for supper, and then her mother will drive me home later. *She* suggested it. Oh, can I go, Mom? I mean *may* I?"

Mrs. Powell shrugged. "Well, all right. Then we'll have Kathy over for one evening."

Tommy could hardly wait till Tuesday came. He could have Wag for a whole evening all to himself.

Finally it was Tuesday, and Tommy asked Mrs. Powell if he could take Wag outside with him. Mrs. Powell must have realized how happy he was to have Wag to himself.

"You certainly may, Tommy," she said. She didn't even ask him where he was going.

Tommy didn't know where he was going either. He just wanted to get outdoors with Wag. Wag was only a pup, but there was no snow and it's always more fun with a dog outdoors.

The October air was nippy. The temperature had dipped below the freezing point the night before, and the sky was cloudy. Tommy dressed warmly and carried Wag outside in his arms.

He put Wag down, and they both ran around for a while. Then Tommy rolled on the lawn and Wag crawled over him and bit his ears. Of course, Wag didn't *really* bite. He didn't hurt at all. He was just having a lot of fun, too.

"Oh, Wag, I sure love you," Tommy cried. "I sure do!"

Tommy thought of the creek. The creek was only a short distance away. It was beyond the fence that marked the Powells' property.

"Come on, Wag!" yelled Tommy excitedly. "Come on!"

Tommy spread the fence apart and crawled through. He ran through a field of frost-nipped alfalfa. Wag came stumbling after him. His long black ears flapped like twin flags, and his tail stuck up high.

Wuf! Wuf!

"You poor little fella," said Tommy. "You have trouble running through this, don't you? Come on. I'll carry you."

Tommy picked Wag up. He carried Wag down to

the creek. The water was crystal-clear and shallow. It looked awfully cold.

Tommy stepped on a shiny flat stone at the edge of the water. His foot slipped! He tried to catch his balance. He couldn't! He fell into the water!

At the same time Wag slipped from Tommy's arms and fell into the water, too.

10

Terror took hold of Tommy as he saw Wag up to his neck in the cold, rippling water. Wag's eyes were large with fright. He was whimpering and turning around in the water, looking for a way out.

"Wag! Oh, my poor Wag!" cried Tommy.

Tommy pushed himself to his feet. He splashed through the water, swooped Wag up into his arms, then stepped onto dry land. Wag's curly fur stuck to his body. Water dropped from him in big drops.

Tommy held him tightly. Wag shook in his arms from the cold. He'll freeze, thought Tommy. If I don't get him dried and warm, he'll surely freeze!

Tommy choked back tears. His teeth chattered. If he didn't get into a house and take off his clothes, he might freeze, too.

Suddenly he thought of David Warren's house. It was closer than the Powells' house. The only trouble was that the Warren house was located on the *other* side of the creek.

Tommy stood a moment. His feet felt like they were caking into ice. He knew he should go home to the Powells. But he was afraid.

He decided to go to David's house. He had to hurry. Chills were going all the way through him.

Tommy ran down along the bank of the creek. He reached the road, crossed the short bridge, and raced to the white house where David Warren lived. He knocked on the front door and stood shivering while he waited for someone to answer.

Mrs. Warren came to the door. Her eyes widened in alarm as she saw Tommy. "Tommy! My goodness! Come inside, quick!"

The instant Tommy was inside, David came running into the living room. He stared at Tommy.

"Let me take the puppy!" he said. "I'll wrap him in a towel and get him warm and dry before he catches pneumonia!"

"David, show Tommy to your room," ordered

Mrs. Warren. "Take off your clothes, Tommy, and put on some of David's. Hurry, young man, before you catch pneumonia, too!"

Tommy dried himself and got into David's clothes. Mrs. Warren gave him a blanket to put around him while he sat in the living room.

David had dried Wag. Now Wag was lying on Tommy's lap, wrapped inside a dry towel. His head was down between his paws. His large brown eyes kept looking around. Every once in a while his shiny nose quivered. His ears jerked. His tail tossed back and forth.

"Tell us what happened," Mrs. Warren said. Mr. Warren was there, too. They listened as Tommy told them about falling into the creek.

"Maybe we'd better telephone Mrs. Powell and tell her you're here," she suggested when Tommy finished. "They must be worried by now, wondering where you are."

Tommy's lips trembled. "Maybe you should."

He was scared, though. Mr. and Mrs. Powell would never forgive him for what had happened. The fall into the creek was an accident, but he had no business going down there in the first place. Just wait till Betty heard about Wag falling into the icy water. What would *she* say?

Mrs. Warren went to make the phone call.

"What do you call Mr. and Mrs. Powell, Tommy?" asked David. "Mom and Dad?"

Tommy shook his head. "No. I call them Mr. and Mrs. Powell."

Wouldn't it be nice, though, he thought, to call them Mom and Dad.

Mrs. Warren returned from telephoning. "Mr. Powell is driving his car over to take you home, Tommy," she said.

"I—I could walk," murmured Tommy. His voice shook. "I'm all right. And so is Wag. We're both dried and warm now."

He took the towel off Wag and put Wag down on the floor. He removed the blanket from around himself and placed it on the chair. He stood up.

"I'm all right, Mrs. Warren," he said pleadingly. "Please get my pants if they're dried. And my coat. I'll put them back on. I'll carry Wag and walk home. It isn't far."

"Don't be foolish, Tommy. It's quite dark out now. Anyway, you wear David's pants tonight. Yours aren't quite dry. Mr. Powell will be here in a minute. He'll take you home. And don't be afraid. He won't be angry. Neither will Mrs. Powell. They're both very nice, understanding folks."

They *will* be angry, thought Tommy. Just wait and see. They'll never forgive me this time.

11

What happened, Tommy?" said Mr. Powell quietly.

They were home, sitting in the living room. Usually the TV set would be turned on at this time of the evening. It was off now. Betty wasn't home yet. Tommy was thankful for that. But she would learn the bad news when she came home, so it didn't make any difference. No matter how he looked at it, he was in a fix.

Why hadn't he stayed in the house and played with Wag? Why?

Tommy looked at the floor. He blinked his eyes and swallowed.

"Maybe you'd rather wait and tell us tomorrow," said Mr. Powell.

Tommy nodded. He didn't take his eyes from the floor. "Yes," he said softly. "Yes, I think I would, Mr. Powell."

"In that case, you should probably go to bed, Tommy," said Mr. Powell. "Get a good night's rest. There's football practice tomorrow, remember."

Tommy raised his head. "Yes, sir," he said. As he got up from the chair, a car drove in the driveway.

"I think that's Betty now," Mrs. Powell said.

A moment later, Betty came into the house.

"Hello, Mom, Dad, Tommy!" she cried excitedly. She ran forward and kissed her mother and father. "I had a great time! Kathy can't wait to come here!"

"Well, that's nice," said Mrs. Powell with a smile.

"Where's Wag?" Betty asked suddenly. She looked around.

"In his house," said Mrs. Powell. "Don't worry about Wag. He's fine."

Betty turned to Tommy. Her eyes searched his closely. "Did you play with him a lot?"

Tommy turned away. His heart began to pound. All at once he felt very lonely again. He wished he had somebody to turn to. He needed help. He needed someone to tell him what to do. What *should* he do? Should he tell the whole story now? Or should he wait till tomorrow?

But why wait till tomorrow? What difference would a day make?

He looked up. He swallowed the ache in his throat. He would tell them. He would tell them everything.

"Yes, I played with Wag," he said. "I took him outside with me. I played with him on the lawn for a while. Then I took him down to the creek. That's — that's where the accident happened."

He paused. He remembered the whole thing very clearly. He could even feel the coldness of the water on his body again.

"I slipped on a flat rock. I didn't know it was covered with ice. I fell. And then Wag fell, too. We both got wet. Then I picked up Wag and ran to David Warren's house, because it was the closest. And because I was scared to come home."

Betty stared at him. "You fell into the water? And Wag fell, too?"

Tommy nodded. "Yes. The Warrens dried us off.

51

They — they were nice."

Then he turned. He walked quickly toward the stairs. He stumbled on the first step, then caught himself.

"Good night!" he yelled over his shoulder, and hurried up the stairs to his room.

12

The Saturday morning sunlight was bright. It poured down on the crowd at the football field. But the air was cold. People were huddled in coats and blankets. The Bullets and the Pirates were lined up, ready for the signal to start. The Bullets wore yellow-and-black jerseys. They were kicking off to the Pirates.

The signal came. A toe met the football a Bullet player held slanted on the ground. The ball rose swiftly and whizzed end over end through the air.

David caught it. He rushed down the field. He dodged, spun, twisted. And then he was tackled on his own twenty-eight-yard line.

The Pirates went into a huddle.

"Get ready, Fred," said David. "We'll try number fourteen."

They broke out of the huddle and trotted to the line of scrimmage. The backfield lined up in T-formation. The quarterback stood behind the center. The fullback stood behind the quarterback, with the two halfbacks on either side of the fullback. Tommy Fletcher was at left end, Nicky Toma at right.

David called signals. "Eighteen! Twenty-two! Six! Fourteen!"

The ball snapped from the center. It thudded into David's hands. David quickly spun around and shoved the ball into Fred Wilkins's hands. Fred raced toward the left end. Tommy blocked his man. Then he charged ahead to block the backfield man running in to get Fred. He lost his breath a moment as a Bullet player blocked him. Fred was tackled.

"We gained three yards on that play," said David breathlessly. "Let's try a pass to Tommy."

The teams lined up.

"Four! Twenty-one! Sixteen!"

The ball snapped from the center. Tommy pushed past his man and raced down the field. His rubber cleats kicked up sod.

Then Tommy turned. The ball was curving down at him. Close by, running with their legs pumping hard, were two Bullet players.

Tommy reached for the ball. He caught it! He brought it against his chest — then fumbled it! The ball bounced wildly on the ground.

The referee picked it up and returned it to the thirty-one.

"Third and seven," said David in the huddle. "Let's make this one good. Number eight! I'll take the ball around the left end."

The Pirates formed a single-wing back formation. The quarterback stood behind center a little farther back than he did when the team was in T-formation. The fullback and the two halfbacks stood at his right.

The ball snapped from the center. Tommy charged forward and held his man with a shoulder block. David swept around the left end. He ran eleven yards and was tackled.

The crowd cheered. First down!

Substitutes replaced men on both sides. Steve Marcham took Nicky's place at right end. A whole new backfield came in. David and the others went out. But Tommy stayed in.

The ball was in the Bullets' territory, on the thirty-eight-yard line.

"Let's get 'em," said quarterback Jerry Miller, who had replaced David. "Let's try number four."

They lined up on the scrimmage line. Jerry called the signals and took the snap from center. Jerry pressed the ball against his stomach and rushed through the right tackle. A two-yard gain .

Second down and eight yards to go. Jerry hurled a pass to halfback Henry Collins. It was intercepted! The Bullet player who caught the ball pivoted and started to run crosswise on the field. Then he charged straight forward. He headed toward Tommy. Tommy went after him. Suddenly a man swept in front of Tommy, blocking him so that he couldn't reach the runner.

Tommy stuck out his foot. The runner tripped and fell.

Shr-e-e-e-k!

The referee shoved out an arm, palm down. A personal foul!

Tommy hung his head. He hadn't thought of what he was doing. He had forgotten about rules. Kids back home used to trip runners a lot, even though they knew it wasn't right.

The referee picked up the ball, stood on the line of scrimmage, and pointed toward the Pirates' goal posts.

"Fifteen-yard penalty for tripping!" he shouted.

Tommy was taken out. Mr. Powell motioned Tommy to sit beside him. Tommy did. He pulled a blanket around him.

"How come you tripped that runner?" asked Mr. Powell. "You know that's illegal."

"I know. I just didn't think," said Tommy.

He was sorry. But what good was it to be sorry now? He had had his chance to make a touchdown when David had thrown him that pass. He had fumbled it. Then, to make matters worse, he had purposely tripped a runner. He knew that tripping players was a penalty. But when he had realized that he couldn't tackle that runner, he just hadn't thought about penalties. He had played so much football without knowing the rules that he had forgotten that you were not allowed to trip. He couldn't tell that to Mr. Powell, though. Mr. Powell would think that he was just making excuses.

The first quarter ended with the ball in the Bullets' possession on the Pirates' sixteen-yard line.

Soon after the second quarter started, more substitutions were made. David and the other backfield starters went in.

"Okay, Tommy," said Mr. Powell. "Go in and send Jack out."

A minute later, the Bullets threw a forward pass that went for a touchdown. A kick between the goal posts gave them the extra point.

The Pirates slumped their shoulders hopelessly.

"Come on!" David Warren shouted. "Let's look alive!"

The Pirates received. They carried the ball back to their thirty-two. They gained five yards on an off-tackle play, then a first down on a seven-yard pass to Nicky Toma.

They moved on down the field, then lost the ball on a fumble to the Bullets.

The Bullets brought the ball back up the field.

They were within five yards of the Pirates' end zone when the half ended.

In the third quarter, the Pirates put on power. They played with all the skill they had. They kept moving like a small army across the white stripes toward the Bullets' goal line. Slowly. Surely. Then— an end-around run by Tim McCarthy scored a touchdown!

But they missed the conversion.

Score: Bullets 7, Pirates 6.

In the fourth quarter, the Bullets showed that they were not going to let the Pirates run over them. They moved up the field, making short gains of two yards, four yards, seven yards. Short gains, but they added up to first downs.

The Bullets crossed the halfway mark into the Pirates' territory. First and ten. Then second and six. Then third and two. Again a first down. Again first and ten.

Then the Bullets' quarterback threw a short pass over the line of scrimmage. It was intended for his end. But another pair of hands reached up to steal the ball. Tommy Fletcher's!

Tommy pulled the ball against his chest and

galloped like a young colt down the field. The Bullets' backs chased after him. Tommy kept running, putting more speed in his legs. The white stripes rolled one by one underneath him. He crossed the twenty, the fifteen, the ten. Close behind him he heard the hard-running footsteps of a Bullet player. Then he felt the player's fingers touching his back.

Tommy gave an extra spurt to his running.

He went over! A touchdown!

This time Fred made the extra point. The Pirates won the game — 13 to 7.

Although he was happy to have made the touchdown, Tommy wasn't as happy as the other members of the team. One touchdown wasn't going to make up for all those mistakes he had made.

13

The football field wasn't the only place where Tommy needed to show improvement. Tommy's schoolwork was suffering. The report card he brought home for the quarter period proved it. Most of his marks were C's. He even had one D. And in the space at the right, where the teacher wrote her comments, Ms. Bleam's smooth handwriting said that Tommy had shown a lot of intelligence in his work at the beginning of the school year, but lately he seemed to lose interest. He could be a good student if he tried.

Mrs. Powell read that and said, "What happened, Tommy? Why have you lost interest in your schoolwork?"

Tommy shook his head. "I don't know," he said. He did know, though. He was worried that the

Powells might not want him after another month or so. How could anybody study and be smart in schoolwork with *that* on his mind?

Mrs. Powell called Ms. Bleam on the telephone. She arranged to talk with Ms. Bleam in person the following evening.

The next night, Mr. and Mrs. Powell left the house after supper. Tommy and Betty stayed home. They watched TV and played with Wag.

"Do you like Ms. Bleam?" asked Betty.

"Sure, I do," said Tommy.

"Maybe you should bring home your books to study," Betty suggested.

"Maybe," said Tommy.

"I do," said Betty.

Tommy didn't answer.

An hour later, Mr. and Mrs. Powell returned. They talked with Tommy in his room.

"School is something we have all attended sometime in our lives, Tommy," said Mrs. Powell softly. "Probably some of the things we must do make us unhappy. On the other hand, many things we do in school make us happy. The important thing is, though, that school prepares us for our later lives.

We grow up and find our way into this big world of ours. We become doctors, or lawyers, or accountants, or painters, or professional football players, or any one of a thousand other things we choose to be. But only if we get the education we need when we're young will we be prepared for the higher education that comes later on."

Tommy drank in her words. His mother had never talked to him like this.

"Both Mr. Powell and I would like to see you grow up well prepared, Tommy. We're both certain you can do better in school, because you have shown us around home that you're a pretty smart young boy. Ms. Bleam thinks that if you study more, your marks will certainly go up. Isn't that what you want, Tommy? To have your marks go up?"

Tommy nodded. But he was thinking, too. You're not going to keep me here, are you? You're telling me this so that wherever I go from here I'll try to behave myself, and study my lessons. You don't really, *really* care, do you? You're just telling me this because in a little while you'll be rid of me. Somebody else will take care of me for a while. You just want me to remember that you have been nice to me. Isn't that so, Mrs. Powell? Isn't that so, Mr. Powell?

They left him and went downstairs. Tommy undressed and went to bed. It was a long time before he fell asleep.

He tried to study harder in school. He brought his books home and studied. One evening he stayed after school and came home on the late bus.

"Where were you?" Mrs. Powell asked worriedly. "Detention?"

"No," replied Tommy. "Ms. Bleam wanted me to stay. She helped me with my lessons."

14

On the last Thursday of October, the Thursday before the last football game, Tommy came home from school and picked Wag up in his arms. Wag licked his face.

Mrs. Powell was busy making supper. She hardly looked at Tommy and Betty as they came in. She said, "Hello, kids," and kept working.

Tommy didn't notice anything at first. Later he realized that Mrs. Powell wasn't humming or singing to herself as she generally would. She was very quiet, as if something was on her mind.

Finally Mr. Powell came home. He was his usual, cheerful self. After greeting everyone in the family he said, "Well, it's our last practice session tonight, Tommy. Ready to go to the field?"

"Anytime," said Tommy.

Mr. Powell changed his pants for an old pair. He put on his sweatshirt and heavy coat. He started to follow Tommy out of the door.

"Oh, Bob?" said Mrs. Powell.

Mr. Powell turned. "Yes?" he said.

Mrs. Powell looked at Tommy and smiled. "Go ahead, Tommy," she said. "Mr. Powell will be right out."

Tommy walked out, closing the door softly behind him. He frowned. What was the matter with Mrs. Powell? What was she acting so funny about? Was she telling Mr. Powell something that she didn't want *him* to hear? Was it something about *him*?

A minute later Mr. Powell came out of the house. He started the car and they drove to the field. Whatever Mrs. Powell had said to him stayed with him. But one thing was sure: He wasn't as happy as he had been when he had first come home from work.

The team practiced forward passes and brushed up on their plays. Mr. Powell explained to the boys a new play he wanted them to try in their final game

Saturday. The play was similar to the end-around that they had used many times already.

The team would line up in T-formation. The quarterback would receive the ball from the center, pivot, and give the ball to the left halfback. The halfback would run to the right and then cut sharply around the right end. In the meantime, each player had to take out his man and block him.

The Pirates ran through the play half a dozen times. Finally two teams were picked. They scrimmaged. They worked the play.

"Good!" said Mr. Powell. "Okay! Let's try some pass plays!"

After an hour of practice, the boys were tired and happy to go home. Tommy bathed and went to the supper table, his hair combed neatly back. He felt starved.

They had ham, potatoes, and peas for supper. Mrs. Powell had baked a chocolate cake for dessert.

At last supper was over. Dishes were done. Tommy went into the living room and sat down. Something was wrong. Everybody was too quiet. He watched television for a while, but he couldn't get interested in the program.

Why was everybody so quiet? Even Wag didn't seem to be filled with the pep he usually had. What was going on?

Tommy looked at Mr. Powell, but Mr. Powell was busy reading the evening paper.

After a while Mrs. Powell came into the room. The paper rustled in Mr. Powell's hands as he folded it and put it down.

Mrs. Powell said, "Tommy, I — I have some news for you."

Tommy's eyes widened. He stood up. "What is it, Mrs. Powell?" He tried to keep from shaking.

"Mrs. Kilbourne called today. She said that she'll be bringing over a married couple Sunday. They want to talk to you. They are interested in adopting a boy about your age."

Tommy's breath caught in his throat. Suddenly what he had wanted to say for a long, long time poured out.

"Why don't you adopt me? I want to stay with *you!* Can't you understand? *I want to stay with you!*"

"I know you do, Tommy," Mrs. Powell said gently. "And we want you, too."

Tommy stared. "You do?"

"Yes, Tommy. But a foster home cannot adopt a child it is boarding. Except on rare occasions."

"You — you mean you can't adopt me even if you wanted to?"

"That's right, Tommy. But we're going to try. We're going to try very, very hard to keep you with us."

15

Tommy went to his room. He picked up a book and sat on a chair. The book was about football. He had read a few chapters of it already and loved it. But he could not get interested in the book now. All that filled his mind was Sunday.

He had tried hard to do the right things. He guessed he did, because the Powells would like to keep him. Only now they probably couldn't, because foster parents did not adopt the children they boarded. *Except on rare occasions,* Mrs. Powell had said. Did that mean that there was a chance they could adopt him?

Presently the door, which Tommy had left partly open, squeaked open wider. Tommy looked up.

"Wag!" he murmured.

Wag trotted into the room. He looked at Tommy

sadly, as if he knew that Sunday might be a tragic day for Tommy.

Tommy picked Wag up in his arms. He stroked Wag's thick shining fur.

"Came to see me before I left, didn't you, Wag?" said Tommy. "You know how I feel, don't you? I hate to leave, but that isn't up to me, Wag. It isn't up to the Powells, either. Because they want me here. It's up to somebody else now, Wag."

Wag licked Tommy's chin. Tommy pressed the puppy against his neck. "Maybe I could take you with me, Wag, if I left. At least, we'd be together, then, wouldn't we?"

Tommy's throat ached. He said nothing for a long while. He just sat and held Wag and did some thinking.

Soon an idea popped into his mind. He would get the Powells something — something to show how he appreciated what they had done for him while he had been with them. Just in case the welfare people didn't let them adopt him. He wished Mrs. Kilbourne had something to say about it. *She'd* let him stay with the Powells.

Mr. Powell had tried to teach him good sportsmanship, too. Maybe I haven't learned much, thought Tommy. But I must have learned *some*.

Where was he going to get the money to buy them a gift, though? He couldn't ask the Powells. He wanted this to be a surprise. And what should he buy them?

What could he buy that wasn't expensive but that all three of them would like?

Tommy thought about those things far into the night as he lay in bed. He watched the moonlight on the window shade. He heard the heavy branches of the big oak tree in the backyard creak from the strong wind.

After school on Friday, Tommy went over to David's house. He told David that a married couple was coming to see him Sunday and that they might want to adopt him.

David stared. "But you don't have to go with them, do you, Tommy?" he asked.

"I suppose not," said Tommy. "But if the Powells can't have me, it makes no difference where I go. I want to get something for Mr. and Mrs. Powell and Betty. They've been very nice to me. I can buy

Betty a doll. But what shall I buy Mr. and Mrs. Powell?"

"Let's ask my mother," said David. "She'll help."

Mrs. Warren was surprised when David told her that some people were coming to see Tommy on Sunday and that they might want to adopt him. "So Tommy wants to buy each of the Powells a present," said David. "What do you think he should get them, Mom?"

She thought a while. "Well," she said, "it depends on how much Tommy wants to spend. How much money do you have, Tommy?"

Tommy blushed. "Nothing," he said. "I don't have a penny."

"Then how —" Mrs. Warren paused.

She smiled. "Tell you what. An advertisement came in the mail yesterday. Let's look through it for ideas. We'll decide what you want for the Powells, then we'll figure on how you will earn the money to pay for it."

They looked through the pages of the advertisement. Finally Tommy decided on a shaving set for Mr. Powell and a set of earrings for Mrs. Powell. They could use those things. A doll for Betty wouldn't cost much. Mrs. Warren added the costs together. The total was much higher than he'd expected.

"Rats!" exclaimed Tommy, his hopes shattered. "I guess I won't be able to buy anything for them. Where will I get that much money?"

"You'll earn it," said Mrs. Warren. "Matter of fact, I know exactly what you can do for a starter. David, take Tommy downstairs with you. Gather up all those cans and bottles. I'll give Mrs. Davis and Mrs. Burling both a ring. I'll bet they haven't recycled their cans and bottles in months. When you boys have everything ready, Mr. Warren will pile it into his pickup truck in the morning and take it to Lewiston for you. How does that sound?"

Tommy smiled broadly. "Sounds great!" he said.

"Okay. Get a move on. I'll make those calls."

Tommy's heart beat wildly. He raced out of the room and down into the basement after David.

16

Early Saturday morning Tommy asked Mr. and Mrs. Powell if he could go to Lewiston with Mr. Warren and David. David had asked him to go along, he said.

"Of course, you may, Tommy," said Mrs. Powell, smiling. "We'll be gone from home for a while this morning, too. We're going to see Mrs. Kilbourne and find out what we can do about having you become a member of our family."

Tommy gaped. "You *are?*"

"Yes. We want you as much as you want us, Tommy. Maybe the welfare people will be kind enough to see things our way, and make all of us happy."

"I — I hope so!" breathed Tommy.

Mr. Powell handed Tommy a duplicate key to the

house, just in case he came home before they did. Then he squeezed Tommy's shoulder playfully. "Be sure you're back by game time."

"I will!" said Tommy with a laugh.

The pickup truck was loaded with cans and bottles.

"How much do you think they'll bring in, Mr. Warren?" Tommy asked anxiously as they drove along the highway toward Lewiston.

"It's hard to tell," replied Mr. Warren.

Mr. Warren drove to the recycling yard. A tall, bushy-browed man stepped out of a small shack that had a sign over the door: OFFICE. Mr. Warren talked to him. Then he unloaded the cans and bottles as the man counted them. The man had a pad and pencil. He wrote figures on the pad each time he finished with a boxload.

Finally all of the cans and bottles were counted. The man figured up the amount. "That's a nice load," he remarked. He told Tommy how much it was worth.

Tommy stared. "That much?" he said.

The man's shaggy brows arched. "That's what it comes to, son."

Mr. Warren grinned at him. "That should do it, shouldn't it, Tommy?"

"You bet!"

In the pickup truck Mr. Warren handed Tommy the cash. "There's your money," he said, cracking a grin. "How does it feel to be a businessman?"

"Good!" Tommy said. "But half the money really belongs to David."

"Well," Mr. Warren said, "I suppose you could argue it that way, but we won't. It's all yours, Tommy!"

"Oh thank you, Mr. Warren! Thank you, David!"

They drove onto the main street in Lewiston. Mr. Warren parked the truck. The two boys and Mr. Warren then went into the store that had mailed out the advertisements.

Tommy bought the doll, the shaving kit, and the earrings. He told the clerk to wrap them up separately.

"May I buy some tags?" he asked Mr. Warren.

"You sure can. Let's get those next door."

Tommy bought tags on which to write names. When they returned home, Mrs. Warren wrapped each gift in beautiful wrapping paper. Tommy wrote the Powells' names on the tags and fastened the tags to the gift boxes.

Then he carried them to the house, unlocked the door, and put the packages in his room.

He played with Wag while he waited patiently for the Powells. At noon the telephone rang. Tommy ran to it, his heart racing with excitement. He picked up the receiver.

"Tommy?" a pleasant voice asked.

"Yes. This is Tommy."

"This is Mr. Powell, Tommy. We won't be home for a couple of hours yet. Get something out of the refrigerator for your dinner. And then go to the football field. I've already talked with Mr. Adams. Okay, Tommy?"

"Yes, sir, Mr. Powell."

"We may have some good news for you, Tommy," said Mr. Powell. "See you this afternoon."

17

The crowd at the football game was the largest Tommy had ever seen. The sun shone brightly. People wore sweaters instead of coats. It was Indian summer weather.

The Pirates were playing the Jets. When the game started, Tommy was on the bench.

The Pirates won the toss. They chose to receive. The teams lined up and the Jets kicked off.

David caught the ball on the twenty. He carried it to his thirty-five. He tried an end-around play, lost a yard, then threw a forward pass to Nicky Toma. Nicky snared it. He galloped for ten yards before a tackler brought him down.

The Pirates rolled on to the Jets' twenty-two-yard line, then were penalized fifteen yards for holding.

Second and twenty-five. The ball was now on the Jets' thirty-seven-yard line.

Mr. Adams sent in Tommy. "Tell David to throw you a pass," he said. "Make it good, fella!"

"I'll try!" cried Tommy.

In the huddle Tommy told David what Mr. Adams had said.

"Okay. Number sixteen. Let's go."

The teams lined up. David barked signals. The ball snapped from the center. David caught it, ran back, and lifted the ball to his shoulder.

Tommy shoved his man aside, then ran past him down the field. Two of the Jets' backfield men started after him. Tommy raced toward the sideline. Underneath him a white stripe flashed by. Then another.

David's hand snapped forward. The ball sailed through the air in a spiral.

Tommy stared. The throw was too far!

Tommy picked up speed. He stretched out his hands. He ran faster — faster! And then the ball was zooming down . . . down.

Faster! Run faster!

The ball struck Tommy's fingers. It bounced up. He had lost the ball!

But, no! There it was, in the air again! He reached for it. He caught it and tucked it safely against his body.

And then his feet couldn't keep up with the forward motion of his body. He fell and rolled over.

The whistle shrilled. The referee trotted toward Tommy and took the ball from him. He moved the ball a few yards in from the sideline, then set it near the ten-yard line.

"Nice catch, Tommy!" yelled David.

"Way to go, Tommy!" cried Tim McCarthy. "Let's go for a t.d.!"

Tommy felt good.

First and ten. David handed a lateral to left half-back Tim. Tim raced around the left end for two yards. Then right halfback Stan Baker took a lateral from David and threw a short pass to Tim. Tim burst around the tackle. A fumble! A half dozen players from both teams leapt on the ball!

Shreeek!

The boys unpiled from the ball. Everyone watched to see who had the ball. The boy on the bottom was a Jets player!

"Just our luck!" yelled Tim, unhappily.

David patted him on the shoulder. "Let's hold 'em," he said.

The Jets lined up for punt formation.

"Block that kick!" yelled David. "Come on, men!"

At left end, Tommy dug his toes into the hard ground. He'd get through. He'd get through to block that kick. The Pirates couldn't lose all that ground after having gained so much.

The Jets fullback stood far back, his shoulders hunched forward, his hands outstretched. He called signals in a sharp, loud voice. The ball scraped the ground as it left the center's hands.

Shoulders hit shoulders. Legs tangled. Rubber cleats dug up hard dirt, crushed it to brown dust.

Tommy pushed aside his man and plunged through a hole. He went after the fullback. The fullback caught the ball. He took a step forward, lifted his foot.

Just then a man threw himself against the ball!

The ball struck his padded shoulder, bounced high into the air, then landed on the ground.

Tommy and two Jets players rushed after the ball. Tommy was there first and pounced on it.

Then the quarter ended.

18

David raced off-tackle in the beginning of the second quarter. He got the ball within two yards of the goal line. On the next play, Fred plunged through the line for a touchdown, then converted for the extra point.

Pirates 7, Jets 0.

Tommy, Nicky, and the two tackles went out. Substitutes went in. The Pirates kicked off. A Jets player caught the end-over-end kick and carried it back to the Pirates' twenty-nine.

As he watched from the bench, Tommy thought, Please, please let the Powells be able to keep me!

A loud outburst from the stands wiped away Tommy's thoughts. A green-and-white jersey crossed the goal line. The Jets had made a touchdown.

They converted for the extra point. Now the score was tied: 7–7.

Tommy went back into the game in the second half. In the huddle, David looked across at him and winked. "Come on! Let's get some touchdowns!" he said in a low voice. "Let's try number one, the play Coach Powell taught us the other day."

The Pirates lined up in T-formation. Signals. David took the ball, pivoted, and handed it to Tim. Tim raced around the right end. A five-yard gain!

The Pirates kept moving down the field. Four yards on an off-tackle run. Two yards on a line plunge. Eight yards on a forward pass. Then the Jets held. The Pirates lost the ball on the Jets' sixteen-yard line.

Now the Jets rolled. Six yards. Three. Five. A pass. A long run.

First and ten. Twenty yards to go for a touchdown.

Another pass. It was incomplete. Second and ten.

The quarter ended.

Substitutions were made on both sides.

The score was still 7–7.

The Jets lost the ball to the Pirates at the start of

the fourth quarter. Then the Jets intercepted a pass and ran the ball to their thirty-five. First and ten. They drove through the tackle and gained two yards. They completed a short pass for six more yards. A line plunge gave them another first down.

The Jets rolled again and got within twenty yards of the goal line. The seconds ticked away fast. Soon the game would be over. The season would be over. Maybe all the good things would be over.

A substitute came in. Tommy went out and sat down on the bench. He wiped his sleeve across his sweating brow.

Suddenly a hand squeezed his shoulder. Tommy looked around.

"Mr. Powell!" he cried. "Mrs. Powell! Betty!" His breath caught. All three were there, standing behind him. They were smiling. And Mrs. Powell and Betty had tears in their eyes.

"Tommy, we have good news!" said Mr. Powell. "We had to see the children's court judge and talk with several people. And then we drove over to those folks who were coming to see you tomorrow. We told them we had filed papers to adopt you, and that you wanted to stay with us. They said it was all right!"

"You — you mean they let you adopt me?"

"Yes. It'll take months before you're legally ours, but at least we know now for sure."

Tommy choked up. He turned and looked at the players on the field through blurred eyes.

"Okay, Tommy! Get in there!" Mr. Adams snapped. "Send Jim out!"

His heart beating fast, Tommy yanked on his helmet and raced out onto the field.

The signals. The snap of the ball. Tommy heard the sounds as if from miles away. His man pushed him back. Tommy almost fell. Then he saw the Jets' quarterback fade back . . . back. Saw his right hand raised, ready to throw a forward pass.

Tommy spun. The pass was meant for his man!

Tommy ran back and chased after the end. The quarterback's arm whipped forward. The ball came flying through the air in a spiral. As it passed over Tommy's head, he leapt. He intercepted the ball! His feet came down to the ground. He tucked the ball under his arm and ran down the field.

From his right, Jets players chased after him like a swarm of bees. The stripes flew under Tommy's pumping legs. He crossed the forty, the thirty-five, the thirty, the twenty-five, the twenty.

The Jets players came closer, closer. The fifteen, the ten. Hands reached for Tommy's jersey. The eight, the seven. Hands touched his back. The six, the five, the four, the three . . .

The hands went around his legs, and brought him down!

A whistle shrilled. Tommy looked up, the ball still clutched in his hands. He saw the referee's arms stretched high in the air.

A touchdown!

Tommy rose to his feet, his chest rising and falling as he breathed.

"That's the boy, Tommy!" shouted David. "We needed that!"

"Thanks, David," Tommy cried. Almost in the same breath he went on, "I have good news, David. I'm not leaving the Powells."

"You're not? That's great! How come?"

"They're going to adopt me."

David swung his arms around Tommy's shoulders. "No wonder you're so pumped up!" he cried.

Fred missed kicking the ball between the uprights. But the game ended with the Pirates winning, 13–7.

Tommy rode home with the Powells.

"That was a beautiful run, Tommy!" Mr. Powell said. "Just beautiful!"

The minute the Powells and Tommy reached home, Tommy ran to his room and brought out the gifts. He placed them on the dining-room table.

"Tommy!" cried Betty. "What have you got there?"

"Presents," Tommy said.

"Presents?"

"Yes. For you, your mother, and your father."

Mr. Powell stared at the package, too. "What's this?" he said.

Then Mrs. Powell came in. She saw the package and made a soft sound in her throat. But she didn't say anything.

Tommy opened the big package, took out the

three gift-wrapped parcels inside, and handed them one by one to Betty, Mrs. Powell, and Mr. Powell.

"These presents are for being so nice to me," he said.

They opened the packages. Betty squealed with delight at her doll. Mr. Powell grinned when he saw his shaving kit. Mrs. Powell opened her little white box. She closed her eyes, smiled, and pressed the earrings against her cheek.

"I got the money from collecting cans and bottles," Tommy explained to them. "The Warrens helped me."

Mr. Powell smiled and ruffled Tommy's hair.

"We have a present for you, too, Tommy," Mrs. Powell murmured softly. She turned quickly and went into the other room. Tommy saw her wipe her eyes.

Soon she returned, carrying a large, white cake. She placed the cake in the middle of the dining-room table.

"There," she said. "For you, Tommy."

Tommy stared at the cake. They must have bought it right after they had known he would be theirs. He read the words written in blue icing on it, and his heart melted.

Welcome home, Son.

He looked at Mrs. Powell, Mr. Powell, and then at Betty. He was so choked up, he couldn't speak.

Everybody's face had the broadest, happiest smile Tommy had ever seen. It was as if all the lights in the whole world were shining on their faces.

Mr. and Mrs. Powell came and stood in front of him. They took his hands in theirs.

"Even though it's not official yet, Tommy," said Mr. Powell, "there's no harm celebrating today, is there? Especially after such a great game?"

Tommy shook his head. A proud grin spread across his face.

"It's sure nice to have a mom and dad again!" he said happily.

The #1 Sports Writer for Kids

Read them all!

All available in paperback from Little, Brown and Company

Matt Christopher

Sports Bio Bookshelf

Michael Jordan

Steve Young

Grant Hill

Wayne Gretzky

Greg Maddux

Ken Griffey Jr.

Andre Agassi

Mo Vaughn

Emmitt Smith

Hakeem Olajuwon

Tiger Woods

Randy Johnson